The Promise

and other poems

Beatrice Holloway

TSL Drama

First published in Great Britain in 2022
By TSL Publications, Rickmansworth

Copyright © 2022 Beatrice Holloway

ISBN: 978-1-915660-18-3

Cover :https://unsplash.com/photos/_1E2D_fwdyY
Images: Beatrice Holloway

Contents

Introduction

You will have noticed that I am a writer, a writer, in the main, of children's books.

As a child, I wasn't that fussy about poetry in school, and yet I quite often surprise myself now as an adult, when with my friends we are discussing prose and poetry, I can often quote some of the poems I had learned in my earlier years. 'The Fairies' by William Allingham - 'Up the airy mountain, down the rushy glen...' and 'A Smuggler's Song' by Rudyard Kipling, 'Brandy for the parson, Baccy for the Clerk, Laces for a lady...' by Rudyard Kipling, spring to mind.

Some of my writer friends write beautiful poetry, in depth, about their inner feelings, that are very moving, but my efforts are not at all so profound. I make pictures with words. Often they do not rhyme, and the rhythm is sometimes broken, so I believe my work may well come into the category of free verse. Two poems in this collection won monthly competitions, 'Different Strands' in February 2021 and 'The Hand of Papa' in June 2022. I do hope you enjoy my modest attempts at poetry writing.

LADDIE - A MONGREL

At night a sudden flash of green
Through the darkness thrusts,
By day, amber pools of trust.
Upon the floor you shed
A coat of white, tan and black.
Your odoriferous bed
A raggy sack.

When young your royal ancestors
Pedigree betrayed.
But their instincts with you stayed.
Over commons you go chasing
Rabbits put to flight,
Canine cousins, casual meeting
A rudder greeting, or
Sometimes an unholy fight.

Upturned roots in suburban gardens,
To all house-callers, frantic antics
A pretence of supreme power.
For strangers - a menacing glower.
Padding round on clumsy paws,
Another flower pot on the floor?
In the street regimental walking,
In the park a game of stalking.

Curled up at last at master's feet,
Running, twitching in your sleep,
A wet-nosed, noisy adorable creature
Your faithful love a redeeming feature.

DANCING IN THE STREET

He danced in the street in his filthy bare feet,
Twirling and twisting like a banshee,
Gyrating his desiccate frame.
And we jeered, and made him our game.

He fell to his knees, gave a mumbled cantation.
Then earnestly cried out his wishes.
H spread out his arms and lifted a fist
To the sun in fruitless frustration.

The dread this evoked among the good folk,
Superstition and horror. They desperately prayed.
The rainmaker solemned – no rain today,
And quietly shuffled away.
An early red dawn, just one thread of cloud
No joy in spectators aroused.
The elders peered down the impotent well,
And gazed at the crops with no swell.

But the thread of the cloud grew with the day,
Then a wispy dust swirl was observed.
The clouds billowed and darkened
As wind, torture-howling unnerved
And to thunder roar villagers harkened.

At last came the rain, fierce and with racket
Accompanied with flashes and crackle
Overflowing the once empty river.
A gift from the heavens, omega delivered.

Our sorrow the rainmaker from our village was driven,
But the man was remembered and swiftly forgiven,
As the rain jived joyfully around our bare feet
We too, though drenched, danced in the street.

THE BEHOLDER'S EYE

Don't tell me trees are a dismissive green,
Go search the glossy livery green
Of holly, laurel and churchyard yew.
The silvery underside of birch
And the citrus smell of lime
In early Spring.

Don't tell me it's just a leaf,
Look at the serrated edge of beech.
Leaves of the plane a whole hand span,
Long slender fingers of the willow,
All with maps of live-giving veins.
A canopy, collectively, of shade.

Don't tell me just ordinary flowers,
Catkins, pussy willow, ladies' candles
And clinging witch hazel
Spiders of a yellow flame.
Look again at orchard blossoms
Pink and red and white
A confetti shower over Springtime brides.

Don't tell me Autumn walks are boring,
When rainbow ticker-tape leaves are falling
And you kick them crisp and crackling.
Hear the clunk of mahogany conkers,
Promises of jam from quince, and
Squishy blackberries stain your fingers.

Don' tell me winter trees are dead,
Stark silhouettes in a steel blue sky
Nursing secretly, securely, a new verdant dress.
New life tightly wrapped against sparkling frost.

And still through all the changing seasons,
The glossy livery green of
Holly, laurel and churchyard yew.

COUNTRY SENSES

Owls tu-hooting
Tractors trundling,
Farmhands whistling,
Wasps threatening,
Ripe corn rasping.
These are the sounds of the country.

Geese skeining,
Dogs rounding,
Snails silvering,
Pigeons pilfering,
Dewdrops jewelling.
These are the sights of the country.

Onions pungenting,
Silage spreading,
Foxes marking,
Cattle steaming,
Milk streaming.
These are the smells of the country.

Rump patting,
Lambs' wool curling,
Trout tickling,
Goats butting,
Nettles stinging.
These can be felt in the country.

Cream strawberrying,
Bilberries staining,
Elderflower champagning,
Apples sweetening,
Beans running.
These are the tastes of the country.

THOUGHTS ON DECEMBER

Mornings of crisp sparkling frost
Bright sunshine belies the cold
That seems to last.
The very last of garden plants
Lose the battle to survive
Give way to tips of peeking bulbs.
Early closing of the day
Draw the curtains, turn on the heat
Shut out the darkness.
Bright lights illuminate the streets.
Every culture seeks to entice the sun,
Gifts, singing, dancing parties, fun
Sacrifice and fire until,
The evidence is clear,
The lengthening day bringing hope
the sun will re-appear.

OCTOBER FOURTH

The doors opened, the quiet released,
Replaced by a cacophony of noisy beasts.
Furry cats on ample laps,
Perfect pedigree gently purring,
Old black toms with thoughts of pairing.
Rabbits, to young chests tightly clasped,
Gently stroking to calm their shaking.
Dogs aplenty, large and small,
Held on leads, tails swishing, wagging,
Delighted by the scents for hunting
Eyeing creatures in the hall.
Fish drifting in crystal bowls,
Fluttering birds with eyes black as coal.
Cavies, intelligent and fascinating,
Bulging cheeks of hamsters munching.
Mice, and rats and gerbils too.
Proud owners, old and young,
Protecting, petting and praises sung.
The church now the local zoo,
All welcomed for St Francis's blessing.

THE OCTOBER WAIT

Small groups of people in twos or threes.
Quiet, but excited, they scan the sea.
Dogs told to sit and kept on leads,
They do their best, leashes strained
 And frantically pull, deprived of a game.
First the dunes, then sandy beaches
Fringed on the sun-kissed ocean,
Stand patient watchers with gimlet eyes
Unsure, maybe - then the cry,
There! There, with fingers pointing
At bobbing black, sleek heads of seals.

The first to arrive, the first of many.
Winter guests swim peacefully
Along the beach then back again,
Searching for the safest place
To birth and nurse their growing young
Of snow white fur.
The tide washes in the mothers-to-be,
It isn't time, and
With low murmurings, return to the sea.

Waiting, fighting bulls seeking supremacy,
To win the favours of the flirt
Gliding round them in serenity.
Twisting necks, avoid the bites,
They sink then surface in an explosion
of water, pressed together - tight.
Waiting for coupling time in Spring.

Patiently waiting, this October morn,
Those on the shore.
Waiting too, the mothers-to-be
As are the bulls in the restless sea.

INCH BY INCH

In the spreading shadows of the scrub
Waited her king and her three cubs,
While she was hidden, tawny coat matching
The dried grasses gently swaying.
Her amber, watchful eyes gazing
At the nervous herd quietly grazing.
Still, so still, silently scanning
For the arthritic old, slowly limping
Or the young buck boldly straying.
Biding her time, she made her selection
And began her stealthy stalking.
Moving, quietly with deliberate steps,
Soft pads, one at a time, slowly advancing.
Stilled, so still as the prey came nearer.
Lowered her body, tasselled tail swishing.
Halted.
The front paws stretched
And down on her haunches.
Confident now and ready to pounce.

IF SUDDENLY

Who knows what fate awaits
Those in their evening years.
So, if suddenly my life runs out of time,
Know that I love you.

If cardiac arrest by my means
Of exit from mortality,
A victim of motorway carnage,
Inclement weather or another's rage.
There'll be no time to say
I love you.

If I should be claimed by big 'C'
Or be diseased of brain Alzheimer's or dementia.
Turn not away,
 Intrinsic in your heart, be sure
You know I love you.

If from pain, I'm never free
And I decide on suicide,
Don't blame or be ashamed of me.
Go on with life and remember
I love you.

OF SOME I KNOW

Do they deserve that inner peace,
I see Sunday worshippers share.
I cannot commit myself,
I must be free
To express how much I care,
For those in desperate need.
I give my time and expertise
As prayer alone I don't believe
Can all suffering be relieved.

These happy, well-fed, well dress
Healthy congregations,
Their love, their help, their support
For members only.
Not wed, divorced, live in sin.
No, we just don't want you in.
Oh yes, they contribute to
Relief in destroyed foreign lands,
Signing cheques – then wash their hands.

One alone showed the way.
Too many interpretations of His word.
No more will I listen to their say.
I know well the Prayer of the Lord,
The ten Commandments, deadly sins,
Psalms and the Creed.
These then shall my guidance be,
And trust my deeds will outweigh,
My miserable faults on Judgement Day.

THE PROMISE

The heartache was unbearable.
To see the world He'd created
Destroyed by those made in His image.
By their greed, lust and corruption.
Just one good man was an exception.
Saddened, His masterpiece had failed,
Decided to end all with relentless rain.
Gave warning to that one good man.
And carefully outlined His plan,
The Ark designed to save the few,
Of every creature gather two.

The earth was lashed for many days,
Monsoon proportions of torrential rain.
Devastated by the destruction, pained.
He made a promise so none may cower.
Across the sky, a coloured bower.
Has mankind's faith been broken?
Was that promise just a token
As people, fearful and confused,
Hear that floods are global news.

DIFFERENT STRANDS

A rope made of twisted strands.
Made strong to withstand
The differing needs of man.
Skipping rope, a deep gorge spanned,
Carrying, lifting, tugs of war just for fun.

Now there is another rope
All are clinging to.
Forged with fear, loss and sorrow.
Each link weakening as sad news follows.
Lockdown now, all promises shallow.

And so the New Year full of promise
To vaccinate the populace.
Wash hands, keep a distance mask your face
And stay indoors, to
Halt the virus that seems to mock us.

To make this rope strong again,
The planet never to suffer again,
Nations unite and problem solve,
We to cherish all and tolerate
To make the world a happier place.

February 2021

AT THE WAKE

I was sorry to hear
You'd lost your husband, dear.
I smiled weakly, gave thanks with a nod.
Lost? Not him, the selfish old sod.
He's not very far
Over there, in the black jar.

What was lost was my life
When he made me his wife.
Come here, go there,
Fetch this and fetch that
Each child was a brat.

But soon for me a new life will begin
I'll scatter his ashes without violins.
But no, that's too good for one who has sinned,
So I'll tip his remains in the small trash bin.

ABANDON SHIP

Lifeboat adrift, and supplies now gone,
Their enemy, the blazing sun.
Skins burned to desiccation.
Their lives, they knew, were nearly done.

One gave a mumbled incantation,
And earnestly cried out his wishes.
Then spread out his arms, and lifted his fists
To the sun in fruitless frustration.

Dawn breaks, just one thread of cloud
No joy in the hapless crew was aroused.
'til soft gentle rain fell to relieve their thirst.
'Tis salvation,' each mouthed - at first.

Now terrified, black clouds, electric blue light,
Thundered an orchestral tympani.
The wind whipped waves, awesome heights
Then plunged to heart- stopping valleys.

The fountain powered down over their heads,
They clung to each other, each knew the dread
Of every sailor at sea.
That their bodies will lie in the ocean alone,
And their watery graves will never be known.

BONUS YEARS

The allotted time is threescore and ten.
Then death's scythe wields the ambushed victim.

From innocent birth to unknowing death,
Dreams, love, laughter, sorrow; until eternal rest.

But there are some who defy that foretold,
Who revel in their secret joys, untold.

They wake and count their blessings day by day,
The special smell of rain and new cut hay.

Glad to see again in every extra year,
The seasonal flowers they hold so dear.

Grandchildren happy in their married bliss,
A baby's toothless smile, a toddler's kiss.

They call this extra, thankful time of theirs,
Their welcome, precious, bonus years.

I SHOULD HAVE KNOWN

I didn't know, you didn't say
How much you loved me.
You, a Victorian son,
Personal emotions, never done.
But I should have known.
Your calloused hands held me tight.
Around me your arms folded
When I was in the thralls of fright.
Spoon feeding me when I was ill,
Penny chocolate bars from the station till.
Early morning cycle rides,
Pointing out nature's delights.
Of you, I stood always in awe,
Of your imposing and stern laws.
It was your sister, when you were gone,
Told how much you loved me.
The signs were there – I should have known.
It's not the words, as your care has shown
That your love for me was always there.
You left, leaving me devastated, sad.
Before I could say, I love you always, dad.

NINETEEN FORTY-TWO

I didn't cry.
You wonder why.

Sanatorium was mother's home,
To gran's in Durham, I had gone.
And dad was left – alone.
I was only nine.
I didn't cry.

Sirens wailed – enemy sighted
Endless falling bombs
Shattering homes every day.
Some of the reasons I was sent away.
I didn't cry.

On Christmas morn
Above a warming range,
China dogs and chiming clock,
A woollen, bulging stocking hung.
Could this, I wondered be for me.

Gran stood by, gave a nod and smile.

AND I CRIED.

WHAT WAS THERE
AROUND THE CORNER?

In those now distant days.
A sweet shop, Major Noones,
And Pocket money gone too soon.
Two builders' merchants, ladders, paint and brushes
They were brothers we're told,
Rivalled, quarrelled over what was sold.
Virgin fields to explore,
'til homes were built, they were no more.

LOST

I'm lost in a confusion of consonants,
And quickly search for vowels to make sense,
And so often I'm wrong –it's depressing.

Given up trips to the theatre
Except musicals I thoroughly know.
And to ballet and opera often I go.

Do I hear your impatience you wonder?
Your tone when you catechize, got your aids?
I nod, you unaware of my dismay.

The lift of your shoulders the closing of eyes,
See your facial expressions, the frowns
Can't you see you're putting me down?

Aids I have yes,
Some sounds, still a guess
Like creaking and squeaking

Sibilant hissing,
And birds cheeping.
All hard to locate.

I don't hear when you call.
I can't hear, I tell all.
I'll shout, the thoughtless reply.

I say, look at me – I read lips.
They smile, start with exaggeration,
That too adds to my aggravation.

To their mouths stray hands flutters
Or they turn away without knowing
I no longer see, hear only mutters.

Yes, I wear aids, gladly.
And hear playground laughter
And groans for a football disaster.

The sighing of leaves,
When the wind passes through.
Night time foxes that bark, I hear too.

The singing of kettles,
The tick of the clock
Backfiring cars deliver a shock.

Senses, sight, smell, touch and taste
Still working and playing their part.
As is my heart.

So patience, I beg if dense I appear
It's simply because
I no longer can hear.

THE HAND OF PAPA

Papa said it was bombs and guns,
And our leaving home was begun
As we joined the scurrying throng,
Anxious, eager to reach the border.
So many, and I was afraid,
And clung to the hand of papa.
He let it slip just for a moment,
I grabbed it back, feared being alone.
But the hand was that of a stranger
Who called out 'Another orphan'
And I was taken out of danger.
Spent the night with crying, sobbing others,
Desperate for papas and mothers.
But in the morning many were claimed,
And I waited and waited but no one came.
Evening now and I lost hope.
Then, just one more searching,
For me at last.
And I was gathered into loving arms,
Safe once again with my papa.

FAMILY TREE

Come take a walk in the garden with me,
Said Granddad when I visit for tea.
We stroll down the path,
Watch birds take a bath,
And pick fat pods of green peas.

Then granddad stops.
Said, look what's grown there!
And I look and look and I stare.
And I laugh and I laugh,
For what did I see?

Bright colours of red, yellow and green,
All hung from a bough,
And I couldn't think how.
Then granddad said, listen.
'tis family tradition.

For every child born into the clan,
Be little lady or wee man.
When grandpa they visit,
And if you don't fidget,
A surprise waits for thee.

And what did I see?
You won't believe me
Magically tied as neat as can be.
I saw - just for me
A lollipop tree.

WHAT IF

Regrets, maybes, or what-ifs,
My early dreams were set adrift.
Scholarships, but no funds,
Medicine research I would have done.
To commercial college I was sent,
Skills I gained used time and again.
But none could kill
Curiosity, and the urge to learn.
Night school, philanthropic gift for the workingman,
Was the first to execute my plan.
English, history 'O' levels I began.
Invited to take Education exams.
Led to a career in science exploration,
Alongside the students, learned my occupation.
The Open University for a second degree.
But now, at last, to ease my needs,
The internet is educating me.
So with time much I have gleaned,
And fulfilled my early dreams.

A BOOK OF MATCHES

The old manor house stood empty, forlorn.
Built long before the boys were born.
They made the grounds their secret play
And lit a bonfire this summer's day.

Fuel was needed for the greedy flames.
Seeking food, they entered the house
Disturbing dust motes and a mouse.
A cupboard door, a window frame.
Sparks spitting from the dragon's mouth.
Too soon the gift devoured and gone.

Down mossy steps with a cautious tread
A lad seeking wood so the fire was fed.
The door behind him groaned, slowly shut,
Not a hint of light through the darkness cut.

He called his friends but they heard 'TEA'
Ran home, so didn't hear his plea.
His fingers found the folded book
Within the covers was the last.
The glorious flame from the treasured match
Showed him exactly the door's elusive latch.

SECRETS

School friends whispered secrets,
And one shared by all in class.
They knew it was you
Who put pebbles in Sir's shoe.
Remember the secrets you made with your child,
A water pistol, a birthday present for dad.
Anticipated fun brought on a smile.
Hogging the secret was such a huge task,
Soon blurted out, but it was a big ask.
But all that was the past.

We learned as we grew older, wiser,
Secrets are best not shared.
Drift away, quarrel with you best friend
Who knows the depth of your inner feelings.
A life, a marriage or friendship destroyed
Depend on them keeping your trust
Once ties of friendship are broken.
Keep close your secrets, do not impart,
Especially those, close to your heart.

NEARLY HAIKU

A summer humming
Pollen from spectrum flowers
Happiness is honey.

Confetti petal
A gentle snowflake adrift
In a Spring sigh.

Gentle soft brushing
Eyelashes on blushing cheek.
A flutter of love.

A LIMERICK

Her hair was not bleached but toned,
Her breasts not pads, but silicone.
The face, though not gifted
Was better uplifted.
La Belle, 'til his beard was full grown.

Acknowledgements

Tons of thanks to my family for their honesty, help and suggestions.

Judy Karbritz Jewish Poetry Society – *Harrow Times* Newspaper. 'For the monthly poetry challenge, for acknowledging submissions and always being supportive and encouraging.

As always, many thanks to Anne and John Samson - TSL Publications, for their unstinting help and guidance.

BOOKS BY BEATRICE

Rhys series

1. Training a Greyhound and Other Troubles
2. Urgent! Pocket Money Required
3. Disasters and Delights of Family Celebrations
4. Enormous Responsibilities
5. The Sometimes Society
6. When Rhys Fell Out a Tree
7. A Question of Girls

Towing Path Tales

1. Towing Path Tales
2. More Towing Path Tales
3. A Particular Year

Adult

1. A Man from the North
2. Archie's Children
3. Elusive Destiny
4. Facts, Folklore and Feasts of Christmas (non-fiction)
5. Retired? You must be joking

Plays

1. A Certain Monday
2. Connie's Lovely Boy
3. From Commoner to Coronet
4. Governed by Magpies
5. In Less than Ten Minutes
6. Plays for Young Actors

www.ingramcontent.com/pod-product-compliance
Lightning Source LLC
Chambersburg PA
CBHW030152200626
46812CB00016B/1816